Camille Sanford
4806 Baker Drive
Everett, WA 98203

Missing Rabbit

by Roni Schotter

illustrated by Cyd Moore

Clarion Books 🌙 New York

Clarion Books
a Houghton Mifflin Company imprint
215 Park Avenue South, New York, NY 10003

The illustrations were rendered in watercolor.
The text was set in 16-point Berling Roman.

www.houghtonmifflinbooks.com

Printed in Singapore.

Library of Congress Cataloging-in-Publication Data
Schotter, Roni
Missing Rabbit / by Roni Schotter ; illustrated by Cyd Moore.
p. cm.
Summary: As Kara divides her time between Papa's house and Mama's house,
she is comforted by the presence of her toy Rabbit.
ISBN 0-618-03432-3
[1. Parent and child—Fiction. 2. Rabbits—Fiction. 3. Toys—Fiction.]
I. Moore, Cyd, ill. II. Title.
PZ7.S3765 Mi 2002   [E]—dc21   2001032569

TWP   10 9 8 7 6 5 4 3 2 1

For Michele Coppola and her son,
Daniel, my sweet inspirations
—R.S.

For Amy
—C.M.

When Kara goes to Papa's house, she and Papa eat noodles. Ooodles of noodles! With lots of cheese, please. Kara always brings Rabbit. He sits *plap!* on Kara's lap in the special seat Papa has made for the two of them. Together with Papa, they sing their noodle song.

Late or early, straight or curly, Noodle! Our favorite foodle!

Kara and Rabbit love to play hide-and-seek with Papa. Sometimes Rabbit is hard to find.

At the end of the day, Kara and Papa snuggle tight together to read stories. Papa's sweater feels woolly and warm against Kara's cheek. Rabbit plops cozy in the middle so he can see the pictures.

When Papa says it's time for Kara and Rabbit to go back to Mama's house, Kara feels happy. Also sad. Rabbit pushes up against Kara's ear and whispers something only Kara can hear. "Where do I live?" he asks.

9

Kara shakes her curly head. She doesn't know the answer. Then Rabbit whispers something more.

"Rabbit says he wants to stay here with you, Papa. He doesn't want to leave. He says he wants to live here in your sweater."

So Papa takes off his sweater, and Kara and Papa put Rabbit inside it. Rabbit's floppy ears and fuzzy head poke through. Rabbit looks funny.

When it's time to say good-bye, Rabbit is the fat round cheese in the middle of Papa and Kara's love sandwich.

When Kara goes to Mama's house, Mama asks her, "How's my curly-headed cabbage?" Kara doesn't answer. She misses Rabbit. She misses Papa.

Mama cuddles Kara close. Together they spy on the sky. The moon is wrapped in soft, thick clouds. It looks like Rabbit in Papa's sweater.

"I miss Rabbit," Kara tells Mama.

Mama phones Papa. Papa brings Rabbit.

Mama cradles Kara and Kara cradles Rabbit. Kara leans her cheek against Mama's pajamas. Mama is smooth and smells like a flower. Together they sing their favorite lullaby.

Close your eyes, go to sleep. While the moon beams, you'll keep Safely dreaming in your bed, Till the sun lifts up its head.

The next day in Mama's morning house, Kara and Mama and Rabbit dance. They whirl and twirl, turn and twist. Then Kara rubs Mama's dancing feet and Mama rubs Kara's dancing feet and Rabbit's feet, too. Together they sing their foot-rubbing song.

When they ache, for goodness sake,
Don't stub 'em, please rub 'em.
Sweet feet. We love 'em!

When Mama does her work, Kara and Rabbit do theirs. Then Mama cooks chicken and rice, and the three of them croon a chicken tune.

Can you find a finer treat than ch-ch-chicken to eat, eat, eat? Ch-ch-ch-ch, ch-ch-ch-ch, Chicken!

On Wednesday it's time to go back to Papa's house. Kara feels happy. Also sad. Rabbit pushes up against Kara's ear and whispers, "Where do I live?" Kara still doesn't know the answer. Then Rabbit whispers something more.

"Rabbit says he wants to stay here with you, Mama. He doesn't want to leave. He wants to live here in your pajamas."

So Mama and Kara put Rabbit in Mama's pajamas. Rabbit looks very tall. He is a long string cheese in the middle of Mama and Kara's love sandwich.

At Papa's house, Kara feels happy. Also sad. There is
no Rabbit on her lap to eat noodles with. There is no
Rabbit to play hide-and-seek with. And there is no
Rabbit to read stories to.

Papa phones Mama. Mama brings Rabbit.

Kara cuddles Rabbit close and holds him tight in her
arms. "Where do I live?" Rabbit whispers in Kara's ear.

This time, Kara knows the answer. "You live with
me," Kara tells Rabbit. "From now on, you will stay with
me and go wherever I go. Otherwise, there will be *too
much missing!*"

Rabbit wants to be in Papa's sweater. Then Papa and
Kara and Rabbit play hide-and-seek. This time, Kara and
Rabbit hide together. Papa laughs when he finds them.

When Mama comes to get Kara, Rabbit is safe in
Kara's arms, ready to go with her to Mama's house.
But Rabbit has another question. He nuzzles close to
Kara's ear. "Where do *you* live?" he whispers.

"What is he saying?" Mama and Papa ask.
"He wants to know where I live," Kara tells them.

Mama and Papa both answer.

"In *my* house sometimes," Mama says.

"In *my* house other times," Papa says.

"But wherever you are, you are always in our hearts," Mama tells her.

"You will always be part of me," Papa says, kissing Kara's nose.

"You will always be part of me," Mama says, kissing Kara's toes. "Do you understand?"

Kara is about to answer, when Rabbit interrupts. "*Where* did you say I live?"

"In my lap sometimes," Kara tells him, "in Mama's pajamas other times, in Papa's sweater the rest of the time."

"But always in your heart?" Rabbit asks Kara.

"Yes," Kara says. "Always in my heart."